DREAMS (CLASSIC COVER EDITION)

NAMAN SHUKLA

Made with ♥ on the Notion Press Platform
www.notionpress.com

I dedicate this novel to my mother and my sister. They always encouraged me to write novels and always stood by me. They never stopped me from my passion and always being supportive. They never put me down. My friends also acknowledged my passion for books and they supported e for these fictional works.

Contents

Foreword

The novel was a great experience and fun to read. Until the very end, I was at the edge of my seat and the story took a right-angle turn when the truth was revealed. Unexpected. Great plotting of the storyline and not forget the complex twists, all of them were awesome. The facts in the novel and the character development were outstanding. Arthur's character was such a mixed feeling that it is kind of difficult to understand or decode him in one go. 'Dreams' is the perfect title for the novel as it conveys the story and shows us the importance of Dreams. It tells us about the advantages and disadvantages of our dreams and how horrific they can appear for us. After reading the novel, I was stunned to know that this novel was written in just 1 month, and still has such a great storyline.

This novel can spill your popcorn and can even blow your mind once you start understanding the characters. The starting and the ending were the most important things to be taken in mind because they made the novella interesting and fun. They are the 'heart' of the novel. Overall, it's a must-read.

~Mr. Shivakant Sharma
Professional Lawyer(Reader)

Preface

'Dreams' is the first ever crime thriller novel I am writing besides fantasy and horror fictional novels. Being a teenage writer and a native Indian, I had a lack of vocabulary and phrasing of words. The novel, 'Dreams' is based on the story of Arthur Coolines, a kind and obliging person who had one dream and that was to meet his grandfather once in his lifetime because he perished when Arthur was a year old and even Arthur didn't know what his grandfather was scrutinized like. Arthur was a local of Illinois, so once while taking a train to Illinois, he falls asleep in the train coach and woke up in a queer place full of surprising elements and horrific architecture. Arthur lingers in a loop and then the story reveals his true intentions to the readers.

I once watched a movie named, Sherlock Holmes and was so obsessed with it that I also wanted to create something just like that. Then, anime like, 'Attack on Titan' and 'Death Note' sparked the idea of this novel and I started to work on it. During the formation of characters, I intended to make Arthur more serious and abrupt but when as the story started to build up, I knew what I needed to do with him.

The story's title, 'Dreams' actually tells us about people's avarice and the sunken dreams they make sometimes. Dreams are something that is correlated to our mind and over which, we don't have any control. Dreams play with our subconscious mind and pilfer the data from our day-to-day interactions to build a world we fantasize about. Arthur had the same crisis which was later on told in the form of psychopathy, but in reality, he was yet another person fulfilling his dreams. The action and the leveling of the story slowly reveal the facts of Arthur's intellect and his comprehensive plans.

Prologue

Everyone has dreams and those dreams lead the small sparkle of light to numerous events. The novel, 'Dreams' is a crime thriller revolving around the story of a 22-year-old man, Arthur Coolines, living in Illinois. Despite having everything, he feels gloomy and mournful for his grandfather who died just a year old, and keeps a dream to meet his grandfather one day, if possible, and wishes to see him once in his life. While taking a train to Illinois, Arthur falls asleep in the train coach and wakes up in a queer place with dead people, colossal gates of hell, and terrific gigantic monsters. After choosing one of the Gates of Fate for himself as per the ritual, he meets his grandfather but lingers in a loop, leading the story into various situations and complex escapades.

The story being in a loop states the ambiance of Arthur and his answers to the circumstances he is lingered in. Undoubtedly, there are possible ways to solve a question, and that's what Arthur does.

Arthur, starting from a normal day-to-day life to hell, then resuscitating back a measly duration of time makes the story knotty and paucity of stoicism.

1

A New Journey

Arthur Coolines, a 22-year-old man with 6 feet of height and a charming face wearing an overcoat over a white shirt and black pants was another animal, who can speak. He was also wearing a black fedora hat and a silver steel watch matching the steel badge on the classic oxford shoes. His personality was kind and pleasant. Arthur was immensely helpful and logical. He had such an alluring face and blue deep watery eyes. He had a hooked nose which was quite matched with his face and silky middle-length flowy hair just improvising his looks. Arthur had everything within him, a nice 2-floor house, money, and a simple job. Everything was in its place. Arthur only had one wish in his mind from childhood, and that was, to see his grandfather once in his lifetime.

When he was 1 year old, his grandfather died due to a brain tumor and at the age of 18, Arthur's parents died in a car accident, too. He had a sister, but she drank poison and died because of depression and domestic violence in her in-law's house. Arthur wasn't able to see his grandfather's face clearly, and so does, all he wanted was to see his grandfather once, even in the dreams. He didn't have any photographs or recordings of his grandfather because all the items got burned in the old house when Arthur used to live with his parents, and even his parents didn't know about the pictures.

That day, with all regrets and disappointment, he went to platform no. 4 of Newdver's Central Station, found near Olhesis Street, London. Arthur went to the platform, sat on the bench with a newspaper, and started to wait for the train. A man approached Arthur, asked for the seat, and sat with him, too. He looked a little in the slightly open newspaper and then asked Arthur about the station he wanted to go to curiously.

"Well, I am going to Carshett town, Illinois" Arthur replied

"Oh, what a coincidence. I am heading there too, waiting for the train. Well, it must be a good journey" The man said excitedly

"Hope so" as soon as Arthur replied to him, the train came to the platform with a loud horn.

It was a big, old steam train. The train's engine was hissing steam out of it. The train stopped at the platform and got break itself with a jerk. Arthur and the other passengers went inside the train coach. The inside was elegant and old too. Arthur took the seat whose number was issued in his ticket, and surprisingly, it was a window seat. He sat on his seat and took out a book from the suitcase he was holding with him. It was a fictional novel; the title goes like 'Cafe Denoir' in it. Arthur started to read the book, and, in just a minute, the train started to move.

Soon, the train caught speed, and Arthur was just engrossed in the novel he was reading. Soon, his eyes started to flutter, and he started to doze off. He slept in the coach, supporting his head with the window bar

2

HALLUCINATION

After complete darkness, Arthur woke up from his sleep and found that the train was standstill at the station. The steam was hissing from it. Everyone in the train coach already vamoosed from it and there was no one left in the coach. It was dark in there. Arthur hurriedly took his suitcase, put over his coat, and came out from the train coach. He saw that the platform was filled with extreme mist which was making it difficult for Arthur to see clearly through it. Arthur sauntered a bit and found a man standing in the middle of the mist with his back turned towards Arthur.

"Hello, sir. Can you please tell me where I am right now and where is the exit?" Arthur asked politely

"Straight then left," The man said in a very strange way

"But what is the name of the station?" Arthur asked calmly but the man didn't say anything and got vanished in the mist after taking a walk

Arthur plodded straight and then took a left as per said by the man and he reached an accessible area, without any mist or strange feeling, and encountered a carriage parked on the road.

Arthur went towards the carriage and asked the carriage driver about the place's information. The carriage driver was wearing a black, old hood-attached piece of cloth, all reaching till the feet of the man. The face was unable to be seen through the hood. He was giving Arthur a horrific vibe.

After asking one more time, the carriage driver said just two words to Arthur, "SIT IN"

Arthur was extremely confused that why he is telling him to get in the carriage, but the driver said that again. Arthur, being a nice person went towards the carriage and was surprised to see that the doors of the carriage opened without anyone's help. Arthur waited for a minute but then went inside the carriage. The door closed suddenly with a loud sound and the carriage started to move. The inside of the carriage was very impressive. The details and designs were over the heels and the seat covers were red, matching the black matte finish. The wooden carvings were outstanding, and the door handle was made of pure gold.

After 2 hours, the carriage ceased and the driver again said two words, not much different than the earlier one, but still effective. Those words were, "GET OUT." as soon as the driver said it, the doors opened automatically and the seat where Arthur was sitting hurled him out of the carriage on the ground and closed again without help. The driver pulled the bridle of the horse and with the carriage, he hastened from the road. Arthur stood up on his legs, and as soon as he turned around, the enormous gate astonished him, and he again fell to the ground. It was a gigantic gate with two guards outside checking something of an extensive line divided into two. The guards weren't normal, they were monsters with gigantic bodies, scary faces, large teeth, and terrific eyes. They were checking some papers from the people standing in line and letting them go inside the giant gate. Arthur too went there and when he put his hands inside the pocket, he felt something. When he took out the thing he felt inside the pocket, he was so shocked to see that it was a piece of paper. It was now Arthur's turn to show his paper.

"Show me the paper," The monster said to Arthur in a cacophonous tone

"H...here it is, sir" Arthur stammered and gave the paper to the monster

The monster read the paper, "Hm, Arthur Coolines, 22 years old, died in a train crash. Alright, go in room 15 C by taking the 4th right from the pathway" and returned the paper to Arthur

Arthur was surprised to see the paper, the accident details, and his death date in the paper. he went inside the gate as per said by the monster and took the 4th right. He saw a colossal castle, dark and gloomy, shattered in many parts and demolished a little bit from the top. The castle was already giving him a horrific vibe. Arthur saw the horde of people there inside the castle. He found a lot of people discussing their lifetime achievements, gloomy days, good days, and how they died. Arthur was concentrating but suddenly, 3 boys came from behind Arthur and surprised him.

"Oh, I am sorry. I didn't want to petrify you" One of them said and helped Arthur to stand up because he fell on the ground

"Yeah, you seemed a bit upset, so we came here to talk to you," 2nd man said "My name is Robby Heifinger"

"Mine is Cillary Newman," the 1st person said too

"And I am Edward Freebie" the 3rd man entered the conversation

"I...I am Arthur Coolines, 22 years old, and according to this paper, died due to a train crash" Arthur replied

"Oh, I died from a grasscutter, Cillary died because he fell in a well and Edward died because he was stabbed by a man and got robbed," Robby said

"Oh, I am sorry" Arthur gloomily said

"No worries, man. Everyone here is dead and died because of some strange reason. You see him" Robby pointed towards a man who was sitting alone "He is Carl, he died because a 10-year-old kid frightened him, and that's why he is upset because now everybody is laughing at him"

"So, where are we?" Arthur questioned Robby

"We...don't know, everyone is clueless" Robby replied

Suddenly, a monster came inside the hall of the castle and told the horde to make a circle around him and stand quietly. He was there to announce something. Everyone made a circle around him, and he started to tell.

"Everyone here is died because of something. According to your daily data, you all have committed horrific sins, and that's why you are here. This is hell. Everybody has 5 minutes to prepare mentally and physically. You all are going into the great hall to choose one of the doors which will decide your punishment for a lifetime. If you choose the door, do it wisely because the punishment will be going to be with you for a lifetime and can't be changed. You can't disagree with your decision once chosen or you'll be punished 100 times much more terrifically. The punishment will be for 20 hours a day, 4 hours for rest, and will continue till your sin meter becomes zero. I hope that you'll attend the ceremony peacefully" The monster said and went away from the castle

Everyone in the room after hearing this news became crazy. They started to run here and there, started to take the stress, and scream. But the only person who was standing still and didn't say a word was Arthur. He froze in his place. After 5 minutes, all the people went into the grand hall where they saw 3 gates consecutively placed beside each other. The doors were looking normal, and the same. Monsters made a line of people and they started to choose the door one by one. No one was able to see what was behind the door. The line started to get smaller and much smaller until it was Arthur's turn. Arthur took a deep breath and went inside door no. 3

He was now standing in a white void. The void was infinite and there was nothing but a plain polished floor. No clouds, green sky, blue water, or greenery. Just white infinite walls. Arthur found out that someone was calling his name repeatedly and again. He turned around and saw a hoary old grey-haired man doddering towards Arthur. He came closer and put both first-hand Arthur's shoulders. He smiled at him and said, "I am your grandfather, Arthur."

Since Arthur had never seen his grandfather or his picture, he didn't understand what the old man was saying.

"I am your grandfather, Arthur. I am Nicole Coolines" Old man repeated once again what he said earlier, but this time it didn't take a second for Arthur to recognize his grandfather and he hugged him tightly. Arthur started to cry. Tears were flowing continuously from his eyes and his eyes became red.

"It's okay, Arthur. Don't cry" The Old man said

"Grandpa, you don't know how much I've missed you. I always thought about you. Today my dream came true, grandpa" Arthur sobbingly said

"I've missed you too, Arthur. When you were 1 year old, you had such a pretty smile. I think it does lose its wideness, right? Keep it as it was. That will surely make me more contented" The Old man replied and then he vanished from the void

The void started to collapse rapidly. Arthur couldn't understand what was happening and he started to fluster. The void collapsed completely and even took Arthur within it.

3

PERISHED

Just after darkness, Arthur snapped from the darkness. His eyes were still red and teary. His eyes started to open slowly. He saw that he was still inside the train coach. The book was in his lap, the suitcase was within him and everyone on the train was still there. After that, the train stopped at the platform of Illinois. Arthur was still sitting because he can't gulp the dream, he saw just a moment before. The man who was sitting beside him stared at Arthur and said, "Did your dream come true?"

Arthur stared at the man with a wide smile on his face and nodded in the gesture of a big, 'YES'

Sometime later, the train stopped at the station. With a loud horn, the train gave a hint to Arthur that his station has arrived and now he must go. Arthur took his suitcase, packed his book, and wearing his fedora went out from the train. Carefully, he placed his suitcase on the table, then taking out his wallet from the back pocket he glared at the shopkeeper. He was standing in front of a large food store.

"How can I help you, sir?" The shopkeeper asked politely and Arthur for a while dozed off because he didn't know what he was going to eat

"Maybe, garlic bread and coffee for sure" Arthur continued "Please add extra sugar to the coffee"

"Will be ready in 5 minutes, you can have a seat right there" Shopkeeper pointed his fingers towards a group of chairs and tables

"Yeah, thanks," Arthur said with a widened smile on his face

"Sir, this can be a little ruffling question, but why are you so happy today? Like I've watched you a lot of time here in the station, always in a gloomy mood and in despair but today you look different" The Shopkeeper asked in an eccentric way

"Well, you know that I don't have anyone whom I can say family," Arthur said "All I have is just money and loneliness, no one to care for me"

"I know that sir. I've seen you for almost 4 years and you've gratefully told me everything" The shopkeeper became quiet as hell and started to see the ground and became teary "you told me about how you lost your parents, your sister, and your grandfather. Your old house ablaze and everything you've told me just shows your braveness, still fighting this emotionless reedy world just for some love"

"You're right, but that's the reason I am so happy today" As soon as Arthur said this, the shopkeeper astonishingly started to see Arthur "When I was coming here from the train, I had a very wonderful dream on between. I first saw a lonely vast platform with a thick blanket of mist on it, then a strange person informed me about the exit. A lot of queer things were happening there. I then saw a very dark and scary carriage with a terrific scarcely visible carriage driver. So, he told me to sit in the carriage, the door opened automatically, I went inside and in 2 hours the carriage dropped me in front of a very colossal door with two guards checking some kind of paper of 2 divided lines full of people. I went in the line too. Then, when I went to the castle, I met 3 very nice and humble guys and talked to them. They were...Cillary, Edward and Robby. All of them were great to meet then we went in front of 3 door which was supposed to choose our fate, I chose the 3rd one and then I entered a void. There, I met my grandfather. He was talking to me, hugged me, smiled at me, and more importantly, I saw his face. I know what he looks like, whether it was a dream I don't care, I am just happy that I saw my grandfather's face once and now I am fulfilled"

"That's awesome, Arthur. That dream must be a sign of God for you that your grandfather is still with you, and he always cares for you from another world" The shopkeeper said excitedly like he was also enjoying and sharing the emotions of Arthur

"Maybe that must be true" Arthur replied with tearful eyes "I am just thinking what about mum and dad, are they delightful in paradise? Are they happy?

"They might be, here, take this special coffee I made for you in celebration of you having glimpses of your grandfather with extra sugar and cream and garlic bread" Shopkeeper propelled the plates towards Arthur

After eating the food and drinking the coffee, Arthur was now contented and filled with energy. He was once again ready to go to his home without having stomach aches and dizziness. He paid the amount to the shopkeeper, greeted him with a handshake as a goodbye sign, and after grasping his suitcase, he went out of the station. Outside of the station, he was walking tremendously fast because he was running late for work, and suddenly, out of nowhere he got hit by a car. It was a large SUV. The car struck Arthur so hard that he flew a little height and then collapsed on the ground. His vision started to appear blurry; he was able to see everyone but couldn't talk. A horde of people started to approach Arthur. Arthur couldn't understand what just happened, he was bleeding a lot from his head. He was able to hear people screaming, running here and there, and calling for help. Ceasing cars and he also saw some of them laughing and just don't give a fuck.

"Is this the end? I this day, why?" Arthur was questioning himself "Maybe, grandfather wants me to look after him in paradise"

"What the fuck, please get a car as soon possible, sir" Shopkeeper precluded a person who was going from there and said "Arthur, you are not going to die. Just get a hold of yourself and be brave. I'll help you; we will get you to the hospital, and you will be able to speak again. Just wait for some time"

"C...C...Conor, I...I...I don't think that I a...a...am going to be a...a...alive. Just w...w.... wanted to say, T...T.... T...Thank you" These were the last words that Arthur said and then, his eyes closed completely. He became pale, all his body became deceased and now, Arthur was gone from this world. He died in the lap of Conor Cluss, a shopkeeper of a normal food store.

"ARTHUR!!!" Conor yelled as loud as he can. His eyes were full of tears, his mouth was quivering, and his heart was shattered. A person just a minute before who was so happy and contented died on his lap. Blood was all over his shirt and he was still holding Arthur's perished body.

4

INTO AN ANOTHER WORLD

Now here, Arthur woke up in the same place as the one he dreamed of. That same platform, dark and empty filled with a thick blanket of mist. The same thing happened again. Arthur saw that same man, he tells Arthur the direction of the exit, and the carriage was parked outside there. Arthur went towards the carriage, and the driver told him 2 words, "GET IN" and Arthur went inside the carriage. After 2 hours, he reached the castle gate, entered through it, and was completely shocked to see the same thing. The only difference was that now the people inside the castle were different. Arthur was seeing this while someone scared him from his back.

"Oh, I am deeply sorry. Didn't want to scare you" A man helped Arthur to stand up. He was tall, ripped, and had long black hair. He had green eyes and an old leather bag.

"It's okay," Arthur said "But, do you know why we are here?"

"Maybe, because we died, but don't know the main purpose" He replied cheerfully "I am Nathan Erweild by the way"

"I am Arthur Coolines" Arthur greeted Nathan peacefully and from the back, two more men arrived

"I am Johnny Semerus, nice to meet you," One of the men said

"And, I am Karan Singhania, nice to meet you, Arthur," An Indian man said and greeted Arthur with a little bow, simply 'Namaste.'

Johnny was short and Karan was tall men. They both have sharp jawlines and frizzy hair. Karan had an alluring face while Johnny had pimples and acnes all over his face. His body was skinny, too. But that doesn't mean that he wasn't nice. He was a well-dressed, groomed, and well-behaved person. So classy and elegant.

"So, how you died?" Johnny asked excitedly

"In a car accident," Arthur replied "It hit me and passed by"

Soon, the monster who came earlier the same way came into the hall, announced the ritual, and invited them into the grand hall. Arthur and the other three went into the grand hall. They all saw 3 doors that were going to decide their fates. So, not wasting any time, Arthur chose the 3rd gate like before. He entered the void as same, met his grandfather, talked with him, and then the void started to collapse. Soon in no time, the void collapsed, and Arthur woke up in his world, just the same as he did earlier. He woke up in the train coach, and the passenger next to him asked the same question about the Dream of Arthur as he did earlier. It was just like copying and pasting.

Arthur went outside from the door; it was just the same. He met Conor, talked with him, and then after eating and drinking coffee, he paid the bill and shared his feelings with Conor. It was a little strange for Arthur too because he did see Conor crying on his death but now Conor was just the same as he was before. Arthur took his luggage and went outside of the platform, as soon as he did, now he didn't get hit by a car. He was shocked, but at the same time, he was happy that now he is alive. He ceased a cab and went inside the cab.

"Where to go, sir?" The cab driver asked politely

"Well, 32 A, West side street, Holy Apartments" Arthur replied and examined the car seat, it was a little torn and old "Please drive as fast as you can"

"I will, sir" The driver stared at Arthur from the mirror "You look somewhat in a hurry, is there anything SPECIAL today?"

"Well, today is a kind of party, so I want to reach earlier so that I can do all the decoration and arrangements" Arthur replied

"Oh, so that is the matter" The cab driver took a bottle of water that was on the dashboard and proffered it to Arthur "You look thirsty, you might need some water. Here, take this"

"Thanks a lot, I just wanted some" Arthur took the bottle of water and after taking a swig and returned it to the driver

Soon, the driver started to give a little more acceleration in the car. The car started to move faster and faster, overtaking others so that Arthur can reach home early. The driver was so assiduous driving the car and it was going smoothly but suddenly from the blind turn, a car came and thus the cab driver turned the steering wheel straight in the right direction as much as he can but then his car got hit by a big truck and after taking 2-3 flips, the car flipped on the ground. Everyone from the street ran towards the flipped car to help the driver and Arthur. The car was mangled, and the driver was all covered in blood but still alive. On the other hand, Arthur was bleeding continuously but he was lifeless. The was dead. As soon as the car flipped, Arthur's head thumped with the car's doorknob and at that time, Arthur died. Now everyone dragged Driver and Arthur out of the car. They took Driver with them to treat him and kept Arthur's perished body on the sidewalk and swathed him with a big piece of cloth.

Here, Arthur again woke up in the same dark lonely platform of his dream. At the time of his death, Arthur knew he was going to die but this was now queer. He was in the train, empty and filled with darkness, Arthur was still alive and didn't have a single wound all over his body. Arthur went out from the train; the platform was still empty and dark. He saw the same person on the platform. This time, he didn't ask him for the direction of the exit. He went straight and took a right. He found the exit at the same place with the carriage standing outside. He didn't ask the driver any questions or even hesitated and went straight towards the carriage. The gate opened for him automatically and Arthur went inside the carriage. The door got closed without anyone's help and then the carriage started to move. 2 hours later, the carriage ceased to move, and the door opened again. This time Arthur asked the carriage driver a quite different and unusual question "Where am I? What is happening to me? Why am I always coming here? Why are you always outside the platform to take me? I don't know anything. Every time I die, I come straight to this platform. Why is this happening to me? TELL ME RIGHT NOW!" Arthur yelled at the driver

"Well, I don't have the right answer for all of these questions right now. But you'll soon find out on your own" The carriage driver said in an anomalous tone and bridled his horse and took the carriage straight in the direction of the dark street

Arthur went towards the colossal gate, went inside the castle, and then met with three other dissimilar people. They were 3, but they looked different, and the names too. One was Oliver, another one was Clark and the last one was Dwayne. The only thing similar was the personality. All of them were showing the same kind of personality just as same as the ones earlier. The monster came inside the castle a minute after, announced about the 3 fate doors, and gave them 15 minutes to prepare themselves. Soon after that, Arthur knew what was going to happen. They reached the 3 fate doors. Monsters divided them into groups and made lines out of them. People started to choose gates one by one. When it was Arthur's turn, Arthur froze there for a second. He thought to himself that if the 3rd gate always takes him into the void, then he must have to choose the 2nd door to take him out of this fucking loop. He chose the 2nd door and went inside it.

As soon as he went inside, he started to fall off. It was like he was falling from a deep dark tunnel; he was falling amazingly fast and then when he was about to touch the ground, he stopped and then fell on the ground. The deep dark tunnel was now gone. It was a very vast jungle area. There were trees all over the place, butterflies flying over the flowers, and rabbits hopping from one place to another. The trees were so tall and green. Everywhere was greenery. Arthur was just acquiring nature when an arrow came from nowhere and slightly passed by Arthur. it was about to touch him. Arthur was startled and fell to the ground due to the sudden appearance of the arrow. Then, from the deep forest and dense bushes, some people came out in front of Arthur. They were sitting on horses and looking like Warriors. They had bows and arrows and swords. They were on a count of 15-20 and from the middle of the horde, a big man on a horse came into the scene who was exactly looking like the leader of them all. He was big, wearing heavy armor, having a long sharp sword, and was wearing incredibly old shoes made up of steel. Arthur was so confused now.

"What were you trying to do?" Arthur yelled

"You seem like a little roach in front of me. And what are those types of clothes? You aren't wearing any armor, huh? Looks like they didn't teach you anything" The big guy said

"What the hell are you saying? Who didn't teach me and what?" Arthur asked rapidly since he was unanswerable

"Don't you dare to understand me a halfwit. I am much greater than you, your runt. I am Gabriel Zvlonsko and the commander of the Gorko Army, and I am not like you, bastard. I am more faithful towards my nation" The big guy replied

"I can't understand what you're talking about" Arthur questioned in a shocking manner

"Well, you don't know, you little Ischrin asshole?" The big guy continued "Or...you want me to slaughter you apart and then you'll tell the truth"

"Which truth?" Arthur asked

"Tell me, what were you doing in my land, huh? Do you think you are the person who can easily inform your clan members about us, huh? Looking at your clothes, you're not a member of an army, so, who the fuck are you?" The big guy gave Arthur a long glare

"I don't know any Ischrin or some other weird stuff. I am Arthur Coolines, and I am from Illinois" Arthur said

"Illinois? What is it? I've never heard of this place" The big guy stared at one of the army cadets

"I've never heard of it too, general" The cadet said

"So, then, where is it located ARTHUR?" The big guy asked Arthur in a suspicious manner

"It's a state in the midwestern united states" Arthur relied on while breathing heavily

"Huh, midwestern united states?" The big guy looked clueless "I think you are making fun of me. You all are just assholes. I am going to cut your head off, chop the pieces of your body into very tiny pieces, and will feed my dogs with it. Cadets, take out your arrows and make 100 holes in his body"

"What, are you joking?" Arthur didn't know what was happening. He was just oblivious, but the cadets weren't. they started to prepare their bows and took arrows, aimed toward Arthur, and started to release them "What the hell are you doing, fucking old man"

Arthur was trying to save himself; he was jumping here and there but some 2-3 arrows did pierce him and now Arthur was out of energy. He fell to the ground on his knees. He was bleeding and the wounds were getting deeper and deeper. Arthur didn't lose his faith. He jumped straight towards the horde and ushed one cadet from the horse. He took his sword and started to fight the others with 3 arrows in his body. He was bleeding continuously, but still, he was fighting. He was cutting every one of them but then suddenly he fell again. It seemed like there was no hope for him to get up again.

Suddenly, a lady from nowhere from the deep forest came in between the fight. She started to fight the cadets and seeing her there, the big guy retreated the cops. The lady was tall, charming, and exceptionally beautiful lady. She was wearing clothes from the medieval period and was looking like a goddess. Her eyes were blue, her hairs were black and long and the gold jewelry she was pairing with the white clothes was just cheery on the cake. She looks towards Arthur who was lying on the ground and trying to stand up. She started to stroll towards him with a straight face.

"Oh, thanks. I don't know who you are, but I am thankful right now. You saved my life" Arthur was just trying to be stood up while the lady came much closer to him and then she kicked her right in the middle of the chest. Arthur fell to the ground "What the hell are you doing?"

"You are a great fighter, but you are a damn fool also. Why you came to Gorko's area? They are dangerous. You might be dead here. And first, who are you?" She said

"I am Arthur Coolines" Arthur replied

"And where you came from. You don't know about the Ischrins and the Gorkos?" She asked Arthur

"I am from...Illinois" Arthur replied to the lady with a strange smile

"And...where is it?" She asked again

"It...is...a hidden village. You didn't hear of it because it's not that popular, but it does exist" Arthur replied intensively

"Oh, that's why I thought why you don't know about the Ischrins and the Gorkos," The lady said to Arthur and took out a medicinal herb and started to put in the wounds

"What are they? Can you tell me, miss..." Arthur stuttered

"I am Lancia Agesthene Ischrin, princess of the Ischrin nation and the daughter of Agesthene Ischrin, the king of the Ischrin nation" The lady revealed her hidden identity

"Oh! I am sorry, princess Lancia" Arthur was clearly showing his horrified face to Lancia

"It's ok, Arthur. Ischrins and Gorkos are two different nations with a dark past. When we were kids, our fathers fought with each other. This rivalry turned into a civil war and soon, the government split the nation into two. That's how Ischrin and Gorko were born" Lancia said

"You said 'OUR,' so who was the other person?" Arthur asked

"Damion Dalschmith, he was the prince of the Gorko dynasty. We were friends. We both grew up together but then this incident happened. this thing divided us, but we didn't cease our conversations. But then, the Gorkos killed my cousin, Jessie. When Jessie died, Ischrins attacked the Gorkos, and then, Damion killed my brother, Alveus. I killed Damion after that. Of course, we were friends, but I can't accept the death of my brother and I'll exterminate each one of them" Lancia replied

"What about now? Are they still fighting?" Arthur asked excitedly

"Well, yes. Gorkos are still trying to invade the castle. They want to capture the Ischrin dynasty. After the death of Damion, the rivalry became deeper and now new rules are made. These rules are extremely strict and the king of any of the dynasties kills the one who disobeys the rule, and you were doing that. If I haven't arrived here at the right time, then you might be dead, and your head is supposed to be hanging on the tree" Lancia yelled

"Are you threatening me?" Arthur questioned

"I am warning you" Lancia replied aggressively

"So, why did you save me?" Arthur continued "Like it wasn't that necessary to help me, besides that, I was a stranger"

"I can't let a stranger die, any more of that, you were a great fighter right there. I want you to fight for my army with the Gorkos and in return, I'll give you what you want" Lancia said

"Whatever I want?" Arthur asked and stared her

"Anything, anything you want" Lancia replied rapidly

"I will tell you..." Arthur was saying his intentions but then he got unconscious and fell on Lancia's lap

"God! Why always me?" Lancia thought to herself and took Arthur with her

After some time, Arthur woke up on a big, beautiful bed. He was in a large room with antique décor items, candles, old curtains, and heads of different animals. The room had a big chandelier and was looking very royal

"Where am I? and why am I completely naked?" Arthur yelled

"Well, I took you here and took off your clothes" Lancia replied and gave Arthur some medicinal pills with water

"Y...you, you took off my clothes?" Arthur asked shockingly

"Yes, I did. And by the way, I didn't see anything. I closed my eyes completely, but I have surely seen that bruise on your waist" Lancia replied

"Yeah, I got that when I was a kid. I fell from a height" Arthur gulped the pill

"You still recovering, you just need to rest and take the medicines on time. Also, understand one thing. You are not my friend, nor my relative, and neither my lover. You are just a warrior I am hiring to fight from my side and if you ever try to betray me" Lancia put a sword on Arthur's neck "I'll chop off your head"

"I...I will never betray you but trust me please, don't unnecessarily put the sword on my neck" Arthur took a deep breath and said terrifically

"Alright," Lancia replied and took back the sword "You just need some rest. So, sleep a little bit after eating your dinner tonight. And tomorrow, I'll wake you up in the morning and will teach you every single lesson of the army"

"Where's the food, I'm starving" Arthur excitedly yelled

In the command of Lancia, two servants came into the room and took Arthur with them after giving him clothes. They took him to a large dining hall which was beautiful and had lots of different decorative items. The chandelier was impressive, and the table was colossal. There was a lot of food on the table. Arthur ate the food heavily and as fast as he can. He ate every one of them. After satisfying his stomach, he went straight into the bedroom and had a snoring sleep that night. Tomorrow morning, somewhat 6-7 O'clock, Arthur woke up and saw Lancia staring at him continuously

"W...what the hell in the world are you doing?" Arthur screeched

"You look cute while sleeping. But I was waiting for you to wake up for half an hour" Lancia replied calmly

"Thanks for the compliment and WHAT THE HELL? You were waiting for me since 5:30, are you crazy?" Arthur yelled

"No, I'm not. And since you woke up, go to the bath place as fast as you can, Arthur. Take a fresh bath and change your clothes. Come here after that, eat breakfast, and come with me. I'll tell you what you need to learn and who will be your mentor" Lancia said

"Alright" Arthur replied with a positive nod and then took a walk toward the bathhouse

it was a very big area filled with lots of water, just like a vast swimming pool. The odor was too good and the sculptures were spitting water continuously filling up the bath. Arthur took off his clothes, took a dive in the bath, and flipped his hair. He was contented. The water was making him relaxed and releasing stress. Everything Arthur was thinking had just gone away and now it was just darkness in front of his eyes with birds chirming sweet smells of flowers, and something bubbly in water. That was strange, those bubbles he saw coming out from the water. It was looking like someone was there inside, but how can it be, the bath was just so deep. As an assumption, Arthur gave a number 60 feet deep it was. That was an architectural beauty. A bath 60 feet deep and was built inside a castle, was just mind-blowing. Soon, Arthur started to think again of the bubbles which were continuously coming in from the water.

"What is it?" He thought "Must be a sort of fish or else"

The bubbles vanished in a moment. It was completely gone. Arthur felt pleased as he was already assuming that there can be no one inside a 60 feet deep bathtub, a wide look-alike of a bathtub. Arthur was just relaxing when the bubbles started to come much faster than before, and in an instant, a colossal giant creature came out from the water. He was something 40 feet long. He was like a giant snake, but he had tiny hands in front like the T-rex. The creature was horrifying and the black color on him was completely terrific. He had big, wide blank white eyes with no pupils. His teeth were as sharp as a knife and were somewhat Arthur's height. One tooth of the creature is of Arthur's height. His snake-like appearance, colossal size, and his roar made Arthur frightened. Arthur started to swim to help himself but the creature attacked him. He was just so close to becoming a snack of a giant snake. Arthur swam to the corner of the bathhouse, took his clothes, and ran out from there. he took on his clothes and with aggression on his face, he started to walk here and there like he was searching for someone. He thumped his feet on the ground. Suddenly he saw Lncia coming from the corridor.

"Hey, did you take a good bath there? I always loves that bathhouse, although I have another one" Lancia said from a distance

"What do you want, huh? Are you willing to kill me?" Arthur yelled

"W...what happened? What did I do?" Lancia asked strangely

"You don't know what you did?" Arthur still screeching in aggression "You sent me in a bathhouse with a giant monstrous creature to get me eaten by him, didn't you?"

"See, I am sorry for that" Lancia apologized with a bow "He is Sulla, my pet"

"What the hell, h...he is your PET?" Arthur became shocked

"Yes, he is. Actually, he was so small when I took him to the castle. I found him when I was so small during the hunting game. He was scared of the people and even he got a wound. So I decided to bring him with me, I aid his wounds and then started to take care of him. He was so adorable and playful. I learned about him later that he is a Grogon" Lancia replied

"What's a Grogon?" Arthur asked curiously

"Grogons are a type of dragon, but they don't spit fire or any other thing. They do have a body of a snake but they can change it to the body of something like a dinosaur and also their blood can make you immortal but only of the golden one" Lancia replied "Sulla is a black Grogon and is one of his kind. He is very rare and that's why I decided to pet him because other people might have killed him if they would found him"

"But why did you send me to the same bathhouse where he was chilling?" Arthur questioned

"Sulla loves water. He wants himself to be cool and chilly but I don't know why he was there. We've already made him another bathhouse but I don't know how he came here because he can never go from one bathhouse to another. The only possibility is that he might dig a hole from beneath the bathhouse and then go there. Again, I'm sorry you suffered the cause" Lancia once again apologized to Arthur

"Alright, fine. But why do you still keep him?" Arthur asked

"Because he might be useful on the battlefield. Whenever the enemy will try to invade the castle, we can use him as a weapon. and even I asked him about this, he permitted us to use him on the battlefield" Lancia replied

"But what do you mean by, Talk to him?" Arthur asked terrifically

"It's because Grogons can speak human language, but only when they find you attractive or caring" Lancia replied Arthur with a smile and took him with herself

"See, what do you think about it?" Lancia took Arthur to a big hall with dining and delicious breakfast on it. The room was huge and the designs were pretty. Arthur was stunned by the view he got at that moment. "This is our other dining room, usually used while eating breakfast"

"Great! This is awesome" Arthur yelled

"Thanks for your interest, I'm glad you loved it. Now sit down and have your breakfast" Lancia said

"Oh, yeah, I forgot about that" Arthur replied to Lancia and munched on the food

"Can you eat it by yourself?" Lancia asked politely

Arthur took the opportunity, and although he was able to eat all the food by himself, he acts like he can't eat the food on his own at that moment because all he wanted was to get fed by some royal person once in his life.

"Um, actually, I can't" Arthur replied

"Ha...ha...ha, okay, I'll feed you then" Lancia giggled and took a spoon filled with custard and started to feed Arthur

"Arthur, it does feel great to get fed by your mother, isn't it?" Lancia asked Arthur with a gloomy face and vanished smile

"I can't tell you, because I don't have parents" Arthur replied calmly

"What? I mean, how?" Lancia yelled

"Actually when I was a year old, my grandfather died and so because of that I even didn't know his face. Then at the age of 18, my parents died in a car accident. My house caught fire and burned completely. I shifted to another house, started to work, and started to live on my own. Soon, I started to make money because of my talent and so thus far, I ended up like this" Arthur replied as calmly as can be

"I am sorry, Arthur. I didn't, mean to hurt you" Lancia said with a culpable face

"Nah, it's okay, Lancia. But, why did you ask me?" Arthur questioned

"You know, Arthur. When I was 4 years old, my mother died due to cancer. She loved me till her last breath. My father raised me with care and love, but you know that every father is busy and being a king gave him a lot of work. He started to get off the network and slowly, he started to get a lot and a lot busy. He does care for me but he can't give me what I want. He can't give me time, love, care, or emotional love. The only thing he can give me is materialistic love or money, a lot. I don't want that, I've never asked for it. But I can't blame him for everything.

When the war started, the nation sure wanted him, and thus he went for the fight. As a king, he always thought about the nation and its people first but he never made attention to me. although I am happy that he is very devoted towards the nation and motherland still, he can give some time to his daughter" Lancia started crying

"Um...Lancia, I think you mustn't cry. Even though you lost your mother and had a father with very little attention, you grew up very well as a well-behaved and sweet person. By just looking at you, I can tell you that you look like your mother a lot, not from the face because I never saw you, but because of the personality, you attain. After losing my parents, I was deeply shattered and heartbroken, but you know, Lancia, everything has been destined to happen. If we cry over things like this, we might end up being a loser. You are the very talented and hardworking lady I've ever met, so, as your friend I want to say that you must go on and you must not give up. I can acknowledge your feeling of yours but I can never accept your failure. So, all I want to say is that be brave and show your father that you grew up just like he wanted you to be" Arthur completed with a contented smile

"I...I think you're right" Lancia sobbed and wiped her tears "I'll do just as you said to me, but wait a minute, when you became my friend, huh?"

"Oh! I thought I am, sorry" Arthur replied remorsefully

"Ha...ha...ha, I was just kidding, Arthur. You sure are my friend, the only friend I listen to" Lancia laughingly said

"That's nice to hear" Arthur replied with a smile and both started to laugh as loud as they can

Then, after eating breakfast. Arthur and Lancia came out from the hall and Lancia held Arthur's hand and took him to give him a tour of the castle. She started to show him everything possible. Firstly, she started with the stable of horses, because for her, it was the most beautiful place in the whole castle.

"So, what is the name of these horses?" Arthur asked Lancia pointing towards the herd of horses

"Well, that one is James, the white one is Chloe, that brownish one is Peter, the dark coffee color one is Argon and that last one is Beciaga, my favorite horse. I always use her for traveling" Lancia replied by pointing toward each horse

"Oh, I like this one," Arthur said and pointed toward Argon

"Nice choice! He is also my favorite" Lancia replied

"Oh, I see" Arthur exclaimed

"These are the best thing that ever happened to me. I bought these horses back when I was 17. I love each of them equally. Every horse has something special in themselves, they never disappoint" Lancia said

"Sure, they don't. Horses or any other animal is more trustful than a human" Arthur delivered a fact

"Sure. Well, so from today onwards, Argon is yours. you can take him with you anywhere you want to go, I am sure he will never disappoint you" Lancia said

"W...what? N...no, I can't take a precious thing from you" Arthur hesitated

"Oh, come on. Please take it. I want you to take him or else I am going to get angry" Lancia threatened Arthur in a playful way

"If you say so..." Arthur muttered and went towards the horse, he touched the horse calmly and started to pat him. His horse also showed love toward Arthur by neighing loudly

"I guess he loves you" Lancia taunted

"Well, I must think that way too" Arthur replied to her with a smile and then they went from the stable to the inside of the castle

The castle from inside was so big and prepossessing and Arthur started to believe that when he visited the weapon room. He stared at the weapons. Everything was fascinating, whether the architecture or the weapons, everything looked flabbergasted. Arthur wasn't able to stop him and ran towards the weapons. He started to examine them much more closely and started to take the feel of every single blade by touching it.

"I am glad you liked it," Lancia said

"I do like them all, they are just awesome. Look at those katanas, the knives, the axes and there are even shields hanging on the wall. I love them all" Arthur happily yelled

"Well, I think you have an attraction toward weapons" Lancia came close to Arthur

"I...I do because all of them look great, aren't they?" Arthur stated

"Yes, they do" Lancia calmly replied "Arthur, whatever blade or sword or axe you like, take it with you"

"What?" Arthur wasn't able to believe what he heard

"Yes, I want you to choose a weapon for yourself so that you can start training" Lancia replied

"Oh, so from where should I start?" Arthur muttered and started to look after every single sword. He tested everyone and after 15 minutes, he found one for himself. It was a very beautiful sword inside a glass cabinet on a velvet cloth. The look of the sword was very royal and even it had gems on it. The blade was so sharp and it hadn't any rust on it. The handle was made of gold and the top of the handle was studded with a big red gem which was alluring and sparkling.

"Great choice, Arthur. That's my great-grandfather's sword. He loved the sword. You can take it out" Lancia pushed Arthur

"O...okay" Arthur slowly took out the sword from the cabinet and after looking closely, he realized that the sword was much more beautiful from a closer look than it was looking before.

After taking the sword, Lancia proceeded to show Arthur the portraits and pictures of the ancestors of the Ischrin nation. She showed him her great great great grandfather, great great grandfather, great grandfather, grandfather, her father, and then her mother. She showed him every single guy from his family, told about them, and even told him about the history and how Ischrins and Gorkos were happily living together. She in detail told him about the war. She told him that Gorkos prince's father and the king, Arnold Waschiho Gorko, and her father were best friends. They all were living nicely when one-day Gorko's cousin tried to sexually abuse her aunt and then her father slapped Arnold. He took it as a disrespect and then he started a war. Lancia's father wanted to make peace so he apologized to him, but he was deeply drowned in his ego, so her father continued the war and this was how they go divided into two different nations.

She took Arthur with him to a very big field, which was a beautiful garden. It was filled with greenery and was shining with the reflection of the sun. the birds were chirping, the flowers were blooming and the dogs were playing. There were rabbits, dogs, cats, horses, deer, peacocks, pandas, and even crocodiles there. they built a pond, especially for aquatic life. She show him a special room that was bound by iron rods like it was protecting something. Arthur went close to the door and then suddenly, something just hopped towards the rods and Arthur fell back on the floor. He saw that it was a big lion. The lion was roaring so loud that even Arthur was scared of him. He was trembling. He didn't expect to see him. The bars were there to protect the outsiders from the lion, not the lion from outsiders. After showing everything to Arthur and explaining every term of the castle, Lancia took him towards another garden-like area where they show a mansion. In front of the mansion, there was a big man, taller than Arthur standing without a shirt and practicing something. He was holding a sword, swinging it in the air and his muscles, oh god, it was just imaginary to Arthur. The man had long hair, but he wasn't able to see his face because he was turned backward and then, Lancia shouted his name. it was, 'Charles'. He turned around and Arthur saw his face, not just saw, he stared at him. Charles was much much handsome and had a lean ripped body. He was tall, ripped, and had beautiful blue eyes. His face was so defined and alluring. He was wearing a necklace too, which had a cross in it.

The man was so into Charles that he almost forgot what he was there. he was just shamelessly staring at him. Charles had long, brown hair which was tied in a ponytail, looking masculine and his biceps were something around 24 inches. Arthur and Lancia went close to Charles.

"Charles, he is Arthur. Arthur, he is Charles" Lancia introduced both of them to each other

"Oh, Arthur. Heard a lot of you. How you lost a battle and how princess Lancia helped you out there" Charles taunted him

"Um...Yeah, she is strong" Arthur replied, he was embarrassed

"So, why you took him here, Lancia?" Charles asked Lancia

"Well, I want you to teach him some basics about sword styles, martial arts, and fighting techniques. He can fight well, but not like a professional one" Lancia replied

"Oh, why needed a tutor, huh? He maybe knew everything, I think he is acting like this, isn't he?" Charles taunted him again

"Well, I am not. And I think you are making things up because you also don't know anything" Arthur taunted Charles back which made Charles completely shocked

"Oh, if that's the case then I'll show you who is weak and who is strong. I'll teach you everything. I don't know what she saw in you but if she has chosen you for the battle, I would like to add one thing. If you going to die in the future, in the battle, or if they use you as bait, I'll never and ever help you, I'll just kill you too. The nation comes first then a weakling" Charles stared at Arthur

"What? I don't want you to help me or anything like that, and time will show you everything who is a weakling or who is a chatterbox" Arthur glared at Charles even more

"Guys, stop it please," Lancia said calmly but they were still staring at each other continuously so she shouted "Don't you understand what I am saying, cut it out"

"Sorry, princess Lancia. From tomorrow onwards, I'll start to teach him from the basics" Charles bowed in front of Lancia

"That will be good, come on Arthur, come with me" Lancia replied and started to stroll

"I'll see you tomorrow, Arthur" Charles gnashed his teeth

"I will be there on time, don't you be late" Arthur replied to Charles and went back towards Lancia

"Why she always chooses me to do stuff like this, I am pissed" Charles muttered and he went back to doing what he was doing earlier

"Don't take him seriously or as a shitty person, he is nice, I swear. He is just, a little shy" Lancia apologized to Arthur

"I am not angry or something, I like that guy. He is good, and I am gonna show him tomorrow who the real boss is" Arthur replied to Lancia as she was looking gloomy

"Well, Arthur" Lancia muttered

"Yes?" Arthur questioned her strangely

"Want to come for a tour, a tour to a very beautiful place, my favorite one?" Lancia asked in a barely audible tone

"Yes, I will. Why didn't you inform me earlier?" Arthur became happy

"Took your horse with you, sit on him and follow me" Lancia replied and ran towards the stable after her, Arthur ran too with a smile on his face

He took Argon as his horse. He sat on him, adjusted himself, and in the command of Lancia, pulled the halter o the horse. Argon started to run, as fast as a car. He was talking with air. Soon, Arthur and Lancia were at the place where Lancia was taking him. It was a large lake, a very beautiful and glistening lake. It was enormous and the trees beside the lake were looking very appealing, too. They both went down from the horses, tied the ropes of the horses, and sat down on the green grass looking towards the lake.

"It is beautiful" Arthur yelled

"Yes, I know it. When I was small, I used to come here with my dad sometimes, when he was a caring one. But after the battle, I never came here before. You know, Arthur. This place reminds me of my mother" Lancia said staring at the lake

"Good for you. This type of place sucks my stress and makes me much happier than before" Arthur exclaimed

"Arthur, after fighting the battle, will you go back to your hometown?" Lancia asked

"I will see about it, there's an excuse for me too well. I have found something close to me in your kingdom" Arthur replied to Lancia calmly

"What? What is it?" Lancia started to tremble

"Well, can't tell you right at this moment, but you'll get to know in the future" Arthur replied as calm as he can be and they both went back towards the castle after looking at the sun going inside the lake

At midnight, Lancia woke up from her nightmare. She was panting so hard. She get off her bed, drank a glass of water, and then she went out of the room. She was strolling when she saw Arthur standing on the balcony and staring at the stars in the night sky. He was so lost staring at the stars. Lancia went towards him and woke up from his continuous staring.

"What are you doing here at midnight, staring at the stars?" Lancia asked

"Oh, so it's you, Lancia. I was feeling a little suffocation so I came here to take a fresh breath but when I saw the night full of stars and full moon, I came here and started to stare at it" Arthur replied

"Okay" Lancia muttered

"And, what are you doing here?" Arthur questioned

"I woke up from a nightmare, so I was taking a walk to fresh up my mind" Lancia replied

"Feels like we both ended up waking at midnight, right?" Arthur said

"Right. Tomorrow, you'll start your training and then after 6 months, you'll attend the biggest battle that ever happened here. Are you ready for it?" Lancia asked

"I am" Arthur replied calmly

"Why you accepted my proposal of becoming a cadet in my army just after asking once? Why didn't you think a bit after my proposal?" Lancia asked curiously

"Because I believe you. Because you seem like a good person to me" Arthur replied

"Hm, thought that you would say that," Lancia said

"Seems like it's been a little late, let's go to sleep, or else we will wake up tomorrow completely being a raccoon" Arthur giggled

"Yeah...yeah" Lancia nodded and they both went to their separate rooms to sleep

The next morning, Lancia came into the room where Arthur was sleeping. He was snoring.

"I didn't want to do this, sorry, Arthur" Lancia muttered and took a bucket of water and she pours it all over Arthur. It was cold.

"What are you doing? Killing me?" Arthur yelled and woke up from his sweet dream

"I am sorry, Mr. Arthur, but it's 5 AM and you need to train yourself, you forgot that?" Lancia replied

"What, this early? You didn't even tell me that you were setting the time of 5 AM" Arthur yelled

"Oh, didn't I? I am sorry, Arthur. Now wake up and be ready. Come near the place where we met Charles yesterday" Lancia said and went out of the room

"Fuck this world" Arthur screeched and went straight out of the room to the bathhouse

After taking a bath, eating delicious brekky, and changing clothes, Arthur came to the place where they met Charles on the last day. He saw Charles there standing just as same as yesterday, half-naked. It was cold that morning, but still looking at him was feeling like he is a real monster, he wasn't feeling anything. Arthur went close to him and greeted him with a smirk.

"So, Arthur the great warrior woke up finally" Charles taunted

"Asshole" Arthur muttered very slowly

"What you say? Say it out loud" Charles said

"Nothing! I said to start soon, or do you just want to chatter, chatterbox?" Arthur replied

"You little shit, okay, took out your sword and show me some moves" Charles shouted

Arthur took out his sword and started to show his moves. He was looking like a douchebag. Jumping from one end to another, doing some random moves, and just swinging the sword randomly.

"Ha...ha...ha, what the hell are you doing, Mr. late?" Charles laughed loudly

"What do you mean?" Arthur asked

"Anyways, let's see your martial arts. Lancia told me that you can do good fighting, so let's see if it is worth it or not" Charles said and went towards Arthur, he took the position for the fight and went for the first move

Surprisingly, Arthur threw him like a bag of sand. Continuously, again and again, and again, he beat the shit out of Charles, and a little later, he completely won the martial art and fighting section. But, he was still a beginner in sword art.

"Okay, I'll teach you how to do it, you just have to focus on the sword, attaining the right position and concentration can make you advanced. You just have to move a leg forward, a little bent and then slash. That's how you can use a sword" Charles showed Arthur the correct way of using a sword

"Okay, I think I get it a little now" Arthur replied and started to learn

They weren't able to understand how the 5 hours went very rapidly. They were shocked. But as a teacher and student relationship, they greeted themselves again and both went to their paths. Arthur came inside the castle where he found that Lancia was sitting on the throne and was looking very stressed, so he went to greet her.

"What happened to you?" Arthur asked

"I got the news today that one of our helper women was killed last night. The killer chopped her into pieces and left her in the room" Lancia replied

"What? Horrible" Arthur yelled

"Yes, that's the same way I thought. But, what I am thinking right now is that who killed her and why like this?" Lancia said stressfully

"Maybe a rival" Arthur exclaimed

"Are you pointing the Gorkos?" Lancia asked

"No, I'm not. I am just saying that it might be some personal issues" Arthur replied calmly

"Might be" Lancia muttered

The next day when Arthur went for the training. Charles started by teaching him the 7 most special sword techniques

"So, you have to hold a sword like this and maintain concentration and you must need t watch every single step of the enemy or the rival" Charles yelled "The 3 most rare and advanced techniques are shadow technique, sun technique, and the energy technique. The other 4 are fire, water, air, and land techniques. These techniques are just easier but the rare ones are a real load"

"So, how to do that?" Arthur asked

"See, for these types of sword techniques, you must have to concentrate fully and also out your energy towards the center of your chest so that you can fully unlock the potential and emit some cool techniques" Charles teaches Arthur about different sword styles and then after some hours, they sat down on the bench to take a little rest because they were completely showered from sweat

"Can I ask you something, Charles?" Arthur asked calmly

"Yes, say," Charles said

"Why you are so desperate about serving the nation and its pride? Why do you always do this type of hard work, huh?" Arthur questioned

"Why I am going to tell it to a stranger and I am doing it because princess Lancia told me to?" Charles exclaimed

"Fine, then. Looks like you only hear Lancia, maybe, you like her, don't you?" Arthur giggled but Charles held his collar and stared at him

"There's nothing like this, you are just misinterpreting it" Charles yelled

"Then what's the matter, why so close to her?" Arthur shouted too

"That's not the matter. When the battle of Ischrins and Gorkos happened, I was fighting from Ischrin's side but I wasn't that much patriot at that time. I was just surviving. I found out that Damion was the one who killed my only lover, Christie. When I find that, I went close to him and slaughtered his head apart from his body" Charles replied

"What? So it wasn't Lancia who killed Damion, it was you? But how? When? And why does she tell me that she killed him?" Arthur was so shocked that now he lost his interest in any other thing

"See, when I slaughtered him, Lancia did see me. She didn't say anything and they came close to me. She took the sword from my hand and once again stabbed Damion with it. She looked at me and said that she will admit the crime over her head" Charles replied calmly

"But why did she do that?" Arthur asked, or screamed

"Because according to the government's policies, only a royal can kill another royal, if a local kills the royal or even the commander of the army, he/she will be punished. The punishment is death, not a normal one though. The guilty person will be slaughtered in front of the whole nation and then will be left alone to get eaten by vultures and crows" Charles completed

"So, does that mean she saved you?" Arthur questioned

"Yes, she does save me. From that day I thought that if she can kill her childhood lover just for the sake of the nation, then why can't I be braver and loving towards my country, that's why I do everything she tells me to do. It's not like I am his servant, she never treated me like one but still, I owe her" Charles replied Arthur with a small smirk and teary eyes

The training and the practice ran for almost 1 week, but the crime rate increased, too. The number of women killed was almost 32 and it was horrible. Killed the same way and no suspect was found. No rivals and even it weren't Gorkos this time

"Then, who?" Lancia yelled stressfully

"Get a hold of yourself, Lancia. There's one person I am suspecting, though" Arthur said

"Who? Tell me quickly" Lancia eagerly asked

"I think it's Alfred Vensmith, I found him roaming a lot at midnight and going into the rooms of woman helpers. I've also seen him coming out of the room with a scared expression" Arthur replied

"Grega!" Lancia shouted and a woman came out in front of her "Call the committee as soon as possible and drag Alfred's ass in the judgment hall right now, go"

"Okay, princess" The woman calmly said and went out of there

After some time, the committee was grouped in the judgment hall. Everyone was there. the whole castle was there. Princess Lancia was the judge. She was sitting on the throne because her father was out of the kingdom for some work and being a princess, it was her responsibility to look after a serious happening. 2 soldiers dragged Alfred with them into the hall. Alfred was the finance minister of the kingdom. He was a short-heighted, nerd guy with weak muscles and a beard.

"This committee is called out here to discuss the case of a rapid increase in the murder of woman helpers of the kingdom. The suspect is Alfred Vensmith. So, tell me, Alfred, did you were the one who killed all of them? We have proof and we have also seen you going into the rooms, so no lie" Lancia yelled

"YES, it was me. I was the one who killed them" Alfred shouted and admitted his crimes

"I knew that. But why did you do that? Why you killed all of them?" Lancia asked

"Because I don't like women. They are always so annoying and weak. I can never accept a weakling. Women are always dependent on others and always greedy" Alfred revealed his true identity

"you little piece of shit..." Lancia muttered "Why did you kill the sister of the commander of Gorko's army, tell me" Lancia yelled again

"What? What are you saying? I didn't kill any other person, and sister of commander, nope I don't. I knew that I knew that it was a lie. I tell you the...." Alfred was continuing to talk while Arthur beheaded him with his sword

"Why did you do that?" Lancia shouted

"Because he admitted his crime and was useless. Also, he was planning to kill you" Arthur replied

"What?" Lancia muttered

"Yes. And what about the thing you said earlier?" Arthur asked

"Someone killed the commander's sister. Her body was found in the area of the Ischrin dynasty. Gorkos are now burning in fire. They are angry. The commander said he will erase the Ischrins. Now, they are coming for the war today itself. We have to prepare ourselves in 6 hours or we will be dead" Lancia cried

"Shit. Okay, I'll tell the others and Charles too. You go and prepare the plan. Take everyone to the secret basement of Ischrin castle you told me about. We will prepare the army and weapons. I'll talk to the king also" Arthur said

"Okay" Lancia replied and took everyone in the castle with her to the secret basement

The basement was made so that no enemies can find it and invade it. It was a super-secret basement made by the former king. Only Ischrins of the castle was aware of that. After announcing in the city, every villager and local came into the castle and went into the secret basement with Lancia. Here, Arthur told everything to Charles, and they started to prepare the army. They prepared weapons, and armor and even hide important documents. After that, they protected the horses and every single animal out there. now they all were ready for the war, but still, they were fewer in numbers.

Soon, the Gorkos were in the territory. They were multitudinous and with higher efficiency weapons. Ischrins knew that they had no match for them but still they were ready.

Gorkos entered the castle, started to kill people, and destroy the castle. They started like a fire in a field. Firstly, not so much but then they went over a thousand kills. The army soon started to die. Everyone was bleeding, corpses here and there, and soldiers with internal organs blasted out of their bodies. Arthur, Lancia, and Charles knew that they were lost, but still, they had hope that there are people saved in the secret basement.

"Lancia, go and check inside the castle. If anyone needs help, give them aid" Arthur yelled while fighting a huge Gorko soldier

"Okay" Lancia ran towards the castle

She went inside checking the soldier's corpses to find an alive one. There were none but the door of the bathhouse was still open. She went inside the bathhouse. She saw something really disturbing. Someone killed Sulla and Sulla was lying dead on the corner of the bathhouse. He was bleeding. The water was filled with his blood and was now red. Lancia couldn't stop herself and started crying. She cried as loud as she can, it was her feelings. Then, she pushed Sulla into the water and Sulla slowly disappeared from the water. It was like a funeral. She came out of the bathhouse to check the secret basement. She was walking in sadness when she saw that there was blood in the path of the basement.

She ran towards the basement, she was out of breath but was still running. She was so close to the basement and then what she saw, she fell on her knees. She was staring without uttering any word. Suddenly from behind, Arthur came inside the room.

"Is everything all right he...?" Arthur was stunned to see the scenery

The basement was filled with corpses of dead people. Villagers, locals, helpers, maids, servants. Minister. Everyone perished. The walls were painted red with blood. Kids with broken limbs, mothers with slaughtered bellies, and men with heads slaughtered from their bodies. It was like a cemetery for a second, no, not that, it was like hell. Lancia was crying out loud. She wasn't able to handle herself. First Sulla the this.

"B...but how c...can they k...kill them? It w...was imp...possible. They didn't know the l...location of the basement" Lancia sobbingly said

"There might be a traitor, we must have to find him" Arthur replied to Lancia and took her with himself

Here, when Arthur went I the battlefield, he saw Charles being stabbed by an enemy from behind 3 times. He was bleeding and fell to the ground. Arthur ran towards him and put him on his lap.

"I...I...I am S...Sorry. I...I wasn't able t...to save them" Charles stuttered

"No, you can't die Charles. You can't!" Arthur sobbingly yelled

"I will. P...please, take c...care of p...p.... prin...cess, L.... L...L...Lancia. good...bye, m...my on...ly f...f...friend" Charles said and died on Arthur's lap

Arthur now stood up, he was looking at the situation. Everyone he loved was dead. Lancia was mentally broken down, Charles was dead, Ischrins was dying and even his favorite horse Argon was killed. He was just thinking when a Gorko came from behind and stabbed Arthur. Arthur turned back and saw his face. He was Dublin Vensmith, brother of Alfred Vensmith. He was an Ischrin. When Alfred was killed by Arthur, Dublin saw everything and from that moment, he built a hatred towards Arthur.

"Y...you traitor" Arthur muttered

"You killed my brother, I'll kill you," Dublin said and stabbed him again and again and again

Soon, Arthur fell to the ground. Dublin was slaughtered too. He was bleeding. Arthur on the other side was seeing

John carrying Lancia and going away from the battlefield. The only thing he was possible to say at that time was, "I...I.... I love y...you, L...Lancia" and he died after that.

5

THE PSYCOPATH

Arthur once again woke up from the darkness. It was the same place. The same platform was filled with fog. Arthur was completely shocked. He went out from the train, he started to stroll on the platform. There was no man like earlier. He went outside and saw that the carriage was standing. He quietly sat inside the carriage and then after 2 hours he went to the gate of hell. There he went inside and after meeting with those 3 friends, he went into the grand hall. It was now his turn again to choose the gate. It was clear to him, choosing the 2nd gate will teleport him to the same world he went to before and the same thing will happen, so gloomily, he chose the 1st gate this time. After choosing the gate, he felt like some vigorous force pulling him upwards. He went into the darkness again and when he woke up, he was in the normal world. This felt different. He was on the train when the train stopped at the station, he went out and met the shopkeeper. After that, he went out and walked home by himself. Soon, he reached home.

He opened the door and then closed it from the inside. He unloaded his luggage and took out another suitcase from under the bed. He took it with him and a mask, too.

He changed his clothes, wore a simple T-shirt and jeans, and then went towards the basement. He opened the gate, went downstairs, opened another gate, went inside, another gate, and then more inside. there, he opened a locker with somewhat 6-7 passcodes and types of locks. He opened the box-type locker. There was a glass fridge inside the box and inside that box, there was a body. A corpse of a dead woman. Completely naked. Arthur took out his suitcase, opened it, took out gloves, and wore it. then he took out the surgical knife from it and he was just about to cut the hand of the woman when he intensively turned around and deeply cut the neck of a person. The person was there to kill Arthur from behind. He was holding a big knife. He was just about to stab Arthur and now he was bleeding continuously from the neck. It was a deep wound. The man fell to the ground. Arthur went close to him, sat down on his knees, and stared at him. He was looking scary there.

"What did you think, huh? Killing me there and sending me again in that loop. I just knew that when I chose the 2nd gate, and I just wanted to confirm it. When I went into that world, I thought to use Lancia but now I love her and that's why I told that person to carry her with him to save her. Everything was planned by me. I killed that helper woman that night when I was wandering around. I saw Alfred roaming around there so I went after him. I saw that he had a little daughter for whom he was thieving snacks and food and secretly parenting her. I threatened him to confess the murder of all the women. Then, I kidnapped Gorko's commander's sister and killed her to start the war. I leaked the information to Gorko by the name of Dublin about the secret basement, Sulla, and everything. I knew that Dublin will kill me and that's what I wanted but not in front of that shitty Charles brat, so I told one of the Gorko soldiers the position of Charles and they killed him. I was the one to send the false message to the king to distract him and kill him between the path. I killed Sulla because I knew that he will be a problem with my plan. Everything was done by me. I understood that this is a loop, the key is my death. Every time I die, I once again fall in the loop so I planned to get killed by Dublin and come here. I knew that you would be coming so I just acted a little bit. Even though I miss Lancia, I'll surely find a way to take her out of the loop and marry her in my REAL WORLD" Arthur completed and smirked at the person. He took the surgical blade and slaughtered the man apart

Now, Arthur again fell into the darkness and when he woke up, he found himself lying inside a glass box with different machines on him and tracking monitors. He took them off, and hide in the corner of the room. When the guards came in, he killed them and after taking their clothes, he went out of the prison he was lying in. yes, it was a prison. The secret police department arrested Arthur and kept in there. the whole loop thing was an experiment by one of the scientists involved with the police.

The next morning, chief general, Jason Zojoiff hurled a newspaper on the table in front of the head of the team, Karl Max, and yelled, "See, this is what you pay when you do not pay attention. Now what we will do, our plan is failed chief"

"We will do something about it, team! Find him" Karl screamed and the newspaper which was on the table fell on the floor

'Arthur Coolines, a 22-year-old psychopath killer broke into the prison and escaped it yesterday. S per data and estimates, he had killed over 140 women in the city and now he is roaming openly. A killer between us is something serious. What we will do now? Is this the end? Is this what police can do?'

That was the thing written in the newspaper's front page headline. Arthur was gone, he was arrested 4 years ago on suspicion of killing his mother, father, and 140 women by the secret police service.

Questions Arrising

What he will do now? What is his plan? How will he reincarnate Lancia in the real world from a dream? Can the police catch him again? Why he killed his parents? Why he was in a loop? Who kept him in the loop?

Everything and every mystery will get solved in the next part. Arthur is on his way to achieving his DREAM.

About The Author

The author of this novel, Mr. Naman Shukla is an Indian horror fictional and fictional novels writer who lives in Bhopal, Madhya Pradesh. The writer studies at Hema Higher School located in Bhopal and is carrying his passion for writing books along with his studies. The writer wrote a horror fictional novel, Starklight published by Notion press in 2021 and now, this is the first time he wrote a crime thriller novel.

Naman is also a Fashion Blogger and a chess player, too. he knows how to look good and due to his ultimate attraction towards chess, he is one of the best plot twist makers along Indian Fictional writers. Naman started writing novels at the age of 14 and still developing more to represent the name of India in the field of Horror Fictional in a foreign land. he devotes his work to the motherland and supports the nation emotionally. Namanlives with her sister and her mother and he is also a Content Creator on social media. "Participating in every field can make a person even much better and experienced", this is what he thinks of life and its survival.

Printed by Libri Plureos GmbH in Hamburg,
Germany

9 798889 756521